Emperor Flood

THE STAR QUEEN

THE STAR QUEEN

by Kim Wilkins

illustrated by D. M. Cornish

Random House 🏠 New York

Text copyright © 2006 by Kim Wilkins
Illustrations copyright © 2006 by D. M. Cornish

Published in the United States by Random House Children's Books,
a division of Random House, Inc., New York.
Originally published in Australia by Omnibus Books, an imprint of
Scholastic Australia Pty. Ltd., Gosford, in 2006.

Random House and colophon are registered trademarks of
Random House, Inc.

Visit us on the Web!
www.randomhouse.com/kids

Educators and librarians, for a variety of teaching tools, visit us at
www.randomhouse.com/teachers

Library of Congress Cataloging-in-Publication Data
Wilkins, Kim.
The Star Queen / by Kim Wilkins ; illustrated by D. M. Cornish. — 1st ed.
p. cm. — (The sunken kingdom ; bk. 4)
Summary: Asa and Rollo, acting on information they received from Ragni,
the sorcerer, sail their invisible ship to Emperor Flood's stronghold,
Castle Crag, to find out once and for all whether their parents are alive.
ISBN 978-0-375-84809-4 (pbk.) — ISBN 978-0-375-94809-1 (lib. bdg.)
[1. Brothers and sisters—Fiction. 2. Magic—Fiction. 3. Kings, queens,
rulers, etc.—Fiction. 4. Adventure and adventurers—Fiction. 5. Fantasy.]
I. Cornish, D. M. (David M.), ill. II. Title.
PZ7.W64867Stc 2008
[Fic]—dc22   2007050750

PRINTED IN MALAYSIA
10 9 8 7 6 5 4 3 2 1
First Edition

For Luka

CONTENTS

CHAPTER 1

FIRE AND FLOOD

Asa woke when the world shook.

She had been sleeping in the soft, peaceful dark. Then came the crack of an explosion, a white-hot flash, and the shuddering of the ground beneath Two Hills Keep. Her eyes flew open and she sat up.

"What was that!" she gasped.

Rollo was climbing out of the bed next to her. Little Una, their baby sister, started to cry.

Asa dashed to the window and threw back the shutters. In the distance, beyond the hills, a fiery light flickered.

Aunt Katla hurried in, closed the shutters, and urged the children back to bed. "Come, come," she said.

"What was it, Aunt Katla?" Asa asked.

"I don't know, and I don't want to know. It was a long way off, and I want you children to go back to sleep."

"It sounded like an explosion," Rollo said. "Do you think it was an explosion, Aunt Katla?"

"Don't worry about it," Katla said. "Whatever it was, you're safe here." She swept Una up into her arms and at once the little girl stopped crying. Asa noticed that her aunt's hands were shaking. "I might take Una into my bed until she settles down."

"Why would there be an explosion?" Asa asked.

"Not another word on it," Katla said. "Back to sleep!" She took Una, closed the door behind her, and left the other two children sitting up in their beds looking at each other.

"What do you think happened?" Rollo asked.

"I have no idea," said Asa. "But Aunt Katla was worried. Did you see her hands shake?"

Rollo lay down and pulled the blankets up to his chin. "I feel frightened, Asa."

"Me too." Her eyes went to the shutters, which were now closed. "But I don't know why."

Neither of them slept well after that. When they came downstairs for breakfast in the morning, Katla was acting as though nothing had happened.

"We have smoked fish and beans for breakfast," she said, smiling happily. Una played with a colored ball on the floor at her feet.

Rollo and Asa exchanged glances.

"Aunty Katla," Asa said, "that explosion we heard last night . . ." Katla's eyebrows quivered and Asa became even more frightened. "What was it?" she asked, her voice tight with fear.

Katla sighed, sat at the kitchen table, and pulled Una into her lap. "I fear it's Flood."

"Flood?" Rollo said. Flood was the evil sorcerer who

had imprisoned the rightful king and queen of the Star Lands—Asa and Rollo's parents—and called up the sea so that half the kingdom was underwater.

"Skalti's gone to the markets to see if he can find any information."

Just then Skalti Wolfkiller burst through the front door. Katla jumped out of her chair and made Una cry.

"Shh, little one," Katla said, bouncing her on her hip.

Skalti bowed his head to the children, then turned to Katla. "It's as we feared."

"Explain what you mean," Rollo said. "What's going on?"

Skalti sat with the children, reaching his hand out to cover Rollo's. "Flood is desperately looking for you. The length and breadth of the land, his spies are calling on suspected allies of your parents. If they don't get the answers they want, they pack the cellars with gunpowder and set them alight. Already five homes have been destroyed this way."

Asa gasped, so shocked that she couldn't speak.

Rollo turned big, dark eyes to her. "Asa? Is this our fault?"

Asa found her voice. "Yes," she said.

"No, no, don't blame yourselves," Katla said.

"There's no point lying to them, Katla," Skalti said sternly. "If they hadn't been spied out near Twistwater Point, Flood wouldn't have been so worried. Perhaps until then he thought they were only little children who could harm nobody. But now he knows you are strong and smart, and looking for your parents."

"Does he want to kill us?" Rollo asked.

"I don't know," Skalti said. "But I think you should—"

His sentence was cut off by a thundering on the door.

Skalti leapt to his feet, his hand on the hilt of his sword. Asa and Rollo grabbed on to one another as Katla cried out, "Who's there?"

"We're here on business for Emperor Flood!" called a harsh voice.

"Let us in!" shouted a second.

"Just a moment," Skalti replied, bracing his back against the door.

"Children!" hissed Katla as she hugged a squirming Una tightly against her. "Go!" She indicated the back window with her eyes.

Asa wasted no time, scampering over the kitchen bench and out the window. Rollo was right behind her. The spies were thumping on the door again, and Skalti called for them to wait. Asa dropped the short distance to the grass and Rollo followed her. They ran up toward the peak of the cliffs. Behind her, Asa could hear the door being forced open—cries and shouts. But she didn't look back. Seconds later, she was scrambling into a cave in the cliff face. Rollo was there a moment later.

He sat heavily on the ground, fighting back tears. "What will happen to Aunt Katla and Una?" he asked.

"Don't worry. Skalti will protect them. It's you and me they're after."

"Well, what are we going to do now?"

"Just sit and wait a few minutes. Catch our breath," Asa said. "Very quietly."

They sat and waited. The waves fell upon the shore below, and Asa could feel the blood in her veins pulsing with them. A strong wind blew off the sea, whipping her hair into her face and stinging her eyes.

Half an hour passed. "Should we go back?" Rollo said.

"Maybe. We could—"

Asa's words were cut off by a loud cracking noise. Another explosion!

"No!" cried Rollo. "Not Two Hills Keep!"

"We have to run," Asa said, getting to her feet. "Quickly."

"Where to?"

"The one place we can be invisible," she said.

"*Northseeker!*" Rollo replied. "Of course."

They left the cave and hit the steep path to the beach. Asa's feet skidded on loose stones, but she didn't dare stop or even look behind her. They got to the bottom of the cliff and raced around the curve of the sand to the inlet, where there was a small pile of colored stones. Rollo always left them there to mark where their invisible ship was moored.

Asa's foot hit the gangplank and the ship appeared in front of her. She and Rollo clambered aboard and pulled up the anchor, and they glided out into the inlet. From here, they could see the plume of gray smoke rising from the place their home had once been.

"They set fire to our house," Rollo said, his eyes brimming with tears.

Asa had to blink back tears of her own. "I hope Aunt Katla and Una got out in time."

"Skalti would have made sure they were safe. Wouldn't he?"

In answer to Rollo's question, Asa spied two figures standing under a spreading sea oak and gazing up the hill.

"There!" she shouted. "Aunt Katla and Skalti!"

"Skalti's got Una on his shoulders," Rollo said. "Oh, I wish we could call out to them."

"Throw something in the water," Asa said.

Rollo felt in his pocket, drew out a colored stone, and threw it in the water with a splash. Up on the shore, Skalti turned. He nudged Katla.

Asa flung open the storage box near the tiller and found a woven blanket of red and gold. She spread it wide and cast it into the water. Katla's face broke into a grin. She waved furiously.

"Take care!" she called. "Be safe!"

Northseeker slipped out of the inlet and onto the open sea.

CHAPTER 2

THE CAPTURE
OF NORTHSEEKER

"Where do we go?" Rollo asked. "The outwaters?"

Asa shook her head. "Too dangerous."

"We can't stay around here. There'll be so many sky patrols."

"We have to think this through," Asa said. "If we stay close to home, there will be sky patrols, you're right. But if we go to the outwaters, there are bad spirits."

Rollo thought hard. "The spirits can see us," he

said, "because *Northseeker* is a magic ship. But the sky patrols can't."

"Unless the rising sun hits our mast."

"So we're actually safer right under their noses."

"That's right," said Asa, pushing the tiller. "We're going to sail right into the center of the Star Lands. There are fewer spirits there."

"Then what do we do?"

"We anchor and wait," she said. "Until it's safe to go home." Her heart fell as she said these words. Her home was gone, and Flood wouldn't stop looking for them. "Can you check our supplies to see if we have food and fresh water?"

Rollo plowed through the storage box. He pulled out a tin of hard biscuits and a cask of water. "That's it."

"One of us might have to risk a trip to the markets," Asa said. "But not yet. I think we should spend at least a day and a night on board. We might be lucky. Flood might decide that it's all too much trouble."

Rollo gave her a wry smile. "We'd have to be *very* lucky, Asa."

As they sailed into the main waterways of the Star Lands, distant green hilltops with small farms perched on them swelled above the water. The crumbling turrets of what had once been mighty castles poked up here and there. Once-noble families now lived in their cramped watery confines.

Here and there, Rollo saw laundry hanging out of the big carved windows, and once he saw a boy sitting on a windowsill, playing a mournful tune on his flute. On the higher cliffs, people had built makeshift homes when the waters had risen. Clay-and-turf huts clustered together on crumbling points, and children played at the muddy water's edge. Above them, the sky was marked by one of the hideous balloons that Flood sent out to spy on everyone. This was what he had done to a beautiful land, where everybody had once had plenty to eat and a say in important decisions that the Star Queen made. Rollo thought about all this as they sailed. For a long time, he had been afraid of the evil sorcerer. But now Rollo realized that he hated Flood more than he feared him.

Another huge explosion broke into his train of thought. Rollo jumped in his seat and Asa shrieked. They turned to see a house reduced to flames and rubble. A woman with two small children seemed to be sobbing as she watched from the water's edge. A short distance away, people were running to see what had happened. But none of them was brave enough to come close and comfort the woman, in case Flood's spies decided their houses were next.

Rollo balled his hands into fists. "It's not fair."

"It's our fault," said Asa.

He turned to her, his mouth set in a hard line. "Is there anything we can do to fix it?"

She was quiet for a long time. The burning house fell behind them, and a cloud moved over the sun. Finally she said, "I know how we can fix it."

"How?"

"We'll go to Castle Crag, Flood's castle," she said slowly. "And we'll knock Flood off the throne, find our parents, and make *everything* right again."

Rollo felt fear freeze his blood. *Castle Crag.* He had

heard stories of it: an army of the night had built it from bad magic in just one day, a hulking black monster looming out of the water. He took a deep breath. Asa was right. They had to go.

"Let me see the map," he said.

While Asa steered, he followed the map. "If we keep sailing, we might arrive at Crag by dawn."

"We have to sleep, Rollo," she said.

"All right, then we'll sail until sunset."

On through the day they sailed. They were both too tense for conversation. But as the sun dipped low in the sky, they began to argue about where they should anchor.

"I think we'll be safe anchoring here," said Rollo.

Asa looked around. All she could see were low hills and open water. "But if we sleep too late, the rising sun might hit the mast, and then the sky patrol will see us. We need to sail back a few miles and drop the anchor where we saw those cliffs."

"But that will make our journey hours longer in the morning."

"I told you when we passed them that we should have stopped there," Asa said.

"I thought there might be more cliffs here."

"You were wrong. You can't read the map properly."

"Then let's keep sailing until we reach some shelter," Rollo said.

"It might be hours away. We need to sleep. Just trust me on this. We should go back."

Finally, Rollo gave in. Asa was older and she was always able to argue better than he could. He felt embarrassed, too, that he had read the map wrong. She was probably right: they should anchor near shelter from the sun, just in case they overslept.

They returned to the cliffs and tucked *Northseeker* into the deep shadow behind a jutting black rock. They anchored and lay down to rest. Rollo watched as the sky darkened and then he gave in to sleep. But the hiss of sky patrols passing overhead kept jolting him awake. All night they patrolled. Flood was searching hard for them. Well, he wouldn't have to look for much longer.

Asa's eyes flickered open on the early-morning sky. She sat up quickly and checked the mast. Yes, they were still in the shadow of the cliff. High up in the sky, she could see two sky patrols. The morning sun glinted off the telescopes of one, and she watched them cautiously. Next to her, Rollo stretched and yawned.

Sssshhhhhhhhhhhhhhhhhhhh. One of the balloons filled with hot air.

"I hate that sound," said Asa. "Like monstrous sick lungs taking a breath."

"They're going to pass right overhead," Rollo said, anxiously glancing at the mast.

"Don't worry, we're protected here," she said.

"They're just so close."

A creaking sound behind them caught her attention. "Did you hear that?" she said, turning.

Rollo turned, too. The black rock next to them was making a strange noise. "What do you think it is?"

Suddenly two gigantic eyes in the rock opened. The whites looked bright against the dark surroundings, and they were pale gray and shot with red veins. The rock grumbled, low and deep in its throat.

Asa cried out.

As the rock creature opened its mouth, its jaw creaked and shuddered. It was yawning. It had crooked yellow teeth of sharpened stone.

"How is it that we slept next to a rock creature all night and didn't know?" Asa said, already reaching for the tiller.

"Asa, we can't move. The sun will catch the mast. We'll be seen."

"We can't stay here. I'll stay in the shadows."

Now the rock creature fixed its eyes on them, its pupils shrinking to tiny dots. A jutting edge of rock creaked to life and unfolded into a huge black arm. Another on the other side. Its arms were closing in on them, moving to crush them.

"Hurry," Rollo said, eyeing the sky patrol almost directly over them.

Northseeker sprang forward. Asa tried to stay in shadow, but the rock creature's heavy hands groped closer and closer. She turned the tiller a fraction more. At that precise instant, the rock creature lashed out with its stone fists. *Northseeker* swerved, but the force of the blow shoved the ship out into the morning sunshine.

Golden light poured down onto the mast, illuminating the ship in sharp detail.

"Quick, *Northseeker*," Asa said, "back in the shadows!"

But it was too late. With a cry of triumph, ropes were cast over the sides of the sky patrol's gondola. They were on their way down.

"Go, go!" Asa urged the ship. She tried to sail it back to shadow, but the rock creature had detached itself and was moving toward them.

"We're not going to make it, Asa," Rollo said, his heart thundering under his ribs.

"Get out, then!" she yelled. "Dive into the water."

"You change into a bird."

"I can't. They know about my raven enchantment. Every sky patrol has nets on board. They'll catch me. Go—*go!* While you can!"

Rollo was frozen with fear.

"Go. *Now!*" Asa screamed.

"Breath of a fish within me!" Rollo called, and dived into the water.

With a huge splash, the rock creature dived after him.

Asa turned, just as two of Flood's spies landed on board *Northseeker*. One took the tiller; the other grabbed her arms.

"What are you going to do with me?" she demanded.

"We'll ask the questions," one said. They bound her arms and hooked her to one of their ropes. Then she was pulled up through the air to the sky patrol as she watched *Northseeker* disappear below her in the morning sun.

CHAPTER 3
UNDERWATER CITIES

Rollo watched in horror from under the sea as *Northseeker* sailed off with a spy at the tiller. The rock creature was swimming toward him, so he couldn't stay to see what happened next. He had to swim—and fast.

He darted through the water. Despite the rock creature's massive weight, it was surprisingly fast. Beneath him, Rollo could see the waterlogged remains

of a farmhouse. He speared down through the water toward it. One of the windows was open, and he darted through the opening and waited inside.

The rock creature stopped at the window. It was too big to fit. One mighty stone arm shot through the opening. Its hand uncurled and swept around, feeling for Rollo. Growing angry, it began to smash through the wood around the window. Its huge hand was pulling the waterlogged wood to pieces. Rollo darted toward the fireplace and peered up the chimney. It looked very dark and narrow.

Smash. Crash.

Behind him, the rock creature was hammering a hole in the wall big enough to fit through. He had to go.

Rollo squeezed himself into the chimney. The bricks inside were slippery with algae. His shoulders became stuck. He wriggled harder, came free, and got a little farther before he got stuck again. The rock creature's arm reached through the bottom of the chimney, grazing Rollo's foot. With all the strength he could gather, Rollo pushed himself forward...then his knee caught. He twisted and again came free. Then he was swimming up and up, and popping out the top of the chimney. He swam as fast as he could, and when he was sure the creature was no longer behind him, he sat on an overturned pig trough on the ocean floor to decide what to do next.

It was clear: their plan all along had been to go to Castle Crag. Asa had been captured, so she would be there sooner than him. He sighed as he realized how difficult it was going to be to swim all the way to Castle Crag by himself. He would have to find the entrance and his way to the dungeons to rescue her. Not to mention the fact that he would be really sick after using his enchantments for such a long time. Ragni had said that he might even die....

Only one thing was certain: if he didn't start swimming now, he wouldn't get there at all. He pushed himself off the trough and started out.

Rollo swam. Around him were the remains of a large town. He followed the main road, between half-destroyed houses, past an empty marketplace, a broken pump, and trees whose leaves had long since died, and drifted away on the tide. The road led him to another town, bigger this time. Huge stone blocks had fallen from the castle and the towers poked through the surface of the water. He didn't stop, but kept swimming, past sunken churches and carts parked on the cobbled road as if waiting for their owners to return. He swam on, but soon began to tire.

So he swam more slowly. Only now he thought he saw shadows. Shadows lurking in the spaces between houses, or behind dead trees, or moving swiftly out of his sight as he turned to look at them. He needed to rest but was afraid to stop in case the shadows caught him.

The muscles in his arms and legs started to burn with exhaustion, but still he kept swimming. It began to seem impossible. He wouldn't get to Castle Crag for days, and when he did, he'd be so sick and exhausted that he would be easy to capture. One of the shadows lurked ahead. Rollo stopped and moved behind an old barrel fallen on its side in the drowned street. The

shadow came closer—two, three of them now. Rollo closed his eyes and waited to be caught.

But nobody touched him. He opened his eyes to see three figures rippling around him. At first he thought they were three men, for they had hands and faces and long, flowing beards. But then he realized that from the waist down these men were fish.

"Sjormen!" he gasped, a stream of bubbles pouring from his mouth. "I thought none of you were left!"

"So the rumors say," said one of the sjormen. His beard was red and he had a kind smile. "But we're not as easy to kill as Flood would have liked."

At the mention of Flood's name, the other sjormen began to grumble and complain.

"The waters were ours once," said one of them.

"But now he's filled them with bad spirits," said the other.

"But we still survive and we hope one day for the return of the Star Queen."

Rollo's eyes lit up proudly. "I'm Rollo, the Star Queen's son."

The sjormen exchanged astonished glances. Redbeard bowed low over his fishy tail. "My lord, it is our honor to serve you." He looked up and met Rollo's gaze. "But how is it that you are deep in these waters, so far from your safe keep?"

Rollo sighed and began to explain. The sjormen huddled in closer to listen. He told them all about Asa and *Northseeker* and the explosions and the rock creature and the sky patrol that had taken his sister away. And then he told them that he intended to go to Castle Crag, but he was so tired from swimming that he thought he couldn't go any farther. As he told this story, he started to cry. He hoped the sjormen wouldn't notice, since the tears slid straight into the water. But they heard the catch in his voice, and Redbeard put his arms around Rollo.

"I'm sorry," Rollo said. "I know I shouldn't cry."

"And why not?" said Redbeard. "There's no shame in crying. There's more shame in feeling nothing. You are a brave lad, Prince Rollo, and we will help you all we can."

Redbeard turned to his companions and they began to converse in a strange language. Some of the words were high-pitched squeaks and some were long streams of bubbles. One of the other sjormen detached a little pair of rusted cymbals from his belt and began to clash and rub them together. An odd metallic sound echoed through the water, far away into the distance.

"What are you doing?" Rollo asked.

"I'm calling my brother," Redbeard said. "He has a boat, an underwater raft. We can take you the rest of the way to Crag."

Rollo smiled. "Really? No more swimming?"

"No more swimming," Redbeard said. "But once you get to Crag, we can't help you anymore. We know of an underwater entrance through the drain system, but none of us will fit through. You'll have to go in alone."

Rollo grew serious again. "The drains?"

"They lead first to the dungeons. I presume that's where you need to go?"

A shadow appeared in the distance. Rollo fixed his

eyes on it, then realized it was four more sjormen, dragging behind them a raft about the size of a door. Redbeard told them what to do in his strange language and then invited Rollo to sit on the raft.

Rollo swam up and sat on it, and they pulled him through the water so fast that he nearly fell off. He decided to lie down instead on his stomach, with his hands gripping the front of the raft. Bubbles fizzed past his ears as they raced through the water. Three sjormen pulled the raft from the front, while four pushed from behind. Their muscular tails swished quickly in time; their long beards streamed beneath them. If he hadn't been so worried about getting into Castle Crag, Rollo might have enjoyed the ride. He thought about Asa, about how much she would love to ride on a raft drawn by sjormen, and his heart felt cold. What if those spies in the sky patrol killed her? What if his parents really were dead and he had no one but Aunt Katla and Una left?

Many hours passed and he dozed for a while, falling into uncertain dreams about rushing water and dark places. When he woke, it was growing dark. The sun sent no welcome shafts of light through the water. It was late afternoon and the sjormen were slowing. Up ahead, Rollo could see the black foundations of Castle Crag.

"We're here?" he said, sitting up.

"Almost," Redbeard said. "I'll take you right up to the drain."

Rollo could see it already: a small, dark hole between the mighty stones. Beneath it a pile of debris grew and spread out on the seafloor. The water above was shallow, and Redbeard was careful to keep his head from poking above the surface. He helped Rollo off the raft and swam with him to the entrance.

"Take this," he said, untying a rope from around his waist. It was silver and green, and Rollo ran it through his fingers curiously.

"It's magic," Redbeard said. "With magic words, this rope will tie itself around whatever your eyes are focused on."

"What are the magic words?"

Redbeard made a noise, one of their odd squeaking words.

"Can you say that again?" Rollo asked.

"Kweee-koo, koo-weee-ince," Redbeard said. "Now you try it."

"Kweee-koo, koo-weee-ince." The end of the rope jumped out of Rollo's hands and, in a flash, wrapped itself around the sjorman's beard. "Oh! Sorry," Rollo said.

"Well, at least we know it works." Redbeard grinned and told him the word that would untie the magic rope. When he was free, he helped Rollo tie it around his own waist. "Now, you can swim right up through the drains. It's tight for a little while, but then it opens out. The drainage system runs through the bottom of the dungeon and there are grates along the pipe. If you go too far, you'll end up in the sewers. Keep checking overhead—and good luck."

Rollo's heart was racing. "Thank you! Thank you for everything."

"You are brave, Rollo. Your parents will be proud of

you." Redbeard turned on his tail and darted away through the water.

Rollo summoned all his courage and swam into the drain.

CHAPTER 4

ON BOARD THE SKY PATROL

As the great balloon rose up into the sky, the spies shoved Asa into the bottom of the gondola. Her shoulder hit the wooden seat, but she didn't make a sound. She intended to tell them nothing.

There were three spies in all: two women and a tall, hook-nosed man. He squatted in front of her, smiling cruelly. "Hello, Princess Asa," he said. "My name is Captain Andlit Krokur."

She gazed at him but didn't say a word.

"Come now, Princess. What's this little game?"

Again she was silent.

"You are Princess Asa, are you not? You wouldn't deny that?"

Asa's heart was thundering, but she would not speak.

Captain Krokur got to his feet. As he did so, the shining knife at his waist clattered against the brass binoculars that hung on his belt.

"I see. You're not going to talk. Well, what can I do about that?" He turned to the taller of the two women. "First Mate Beini, let's go to River Hill."

"But, Captain Krokur, we've found them now. River Hill is miles in the other direction, and we don't need to—"

"I said River Hill. Let's fulfill our original engagement there."

Beini shrugged, and she and the other spy began to tug on ropes and wind the wheel on the hot-air machine. They moved swiftly through the sky.

Asa watched the clouds skim past above her and

wondered what was at River Hill. At least they weren't taking her to Castle Crag. As soon as they landed, she would have a chance to break free and run. She was already loosening the ropes around her wrists, clenching and unclenching her fists so that the knots began to slip against each other. The hiss of the hot air was deafening this close, and she couldn't hear what the spies were saying to each other. It was clear, though, that Captain Krokur was giving orders of some sort. The two women nodded. After a couple of hours had passed, one of them came to tighten the wheel on the hot air, and the balloon began to descend. Just before the gondola hit the ground, Krokur himself seized Asa and pulled her to her feet. She struggled, but he was too strong. There was no way he was going to let her go.

"You know what to do," he said to the others.

They nodded. Beini hitched a big white bag over her shoulder while the other woman collected a roll of wire. Then they both climbed out of the gondola and headed up the hill toward a little cottage. Asa frowned, suspicious. But she was determined to keep her silence.

"Ah, there they go, off on Emperor Flood's business," Captain Krokur said. "Don't you wonder what they're doing?"

Asa refused to meet his eye.

"They're looking for the son and daughter of the Star Queen."

Asa's pulse quickened.

"As we haven't found them yet. At least, I don't *think* we've found them. For surely, if you really were Princess Asa, you would have admitted it by now."

Asa watched as Beini and her companion broke down the door of the cottage. A woman holding a little boy about Una's age shrieked and ran from the house. Beini dropped the big white sack and began to pull out fat red sticks.

"Explosives," Krokur said. "If we can't find the children in this cottage, then we'll blow it up." As he turned to Asa, he leaned so close that his hot breath tickled her ear. "I know that Princess Asa wouldn't want that to happen. But perhaps you're not Princess Asa at all."

Asa's eyes widened. The other spy was unraveling the coil of wire. They were getting ready to destroy the woman's home.

But she couldn't let it happen. "Stop!" she said. "Stop them at once."

"Oh, you have a voice?"

"Stop them!"

"No, I won't stop them until you tell me who you are."

Asa glanced wildly from Krokur's ugly face to the weeping woman with the small child. She licked her lips, took a quick breath. "I'm Asa," she said.

"And the young man with you on the invisible ship?"

"Nobody. A boy I found drifting at sea."

Krokur rolled his eyes. "Princess, I'm no fool. One word from me will prevent the explosion. But if you don't cooperate..." He paused for a moment, then shouted, "BANG!"

"All right, all right," she said. "It was my brother, Prince Rollo. We're the Star Queen's children, and you don't have to destroy any more good people's homes. You found me."

Without loosening his iron grip around her wrists, Krokur bent over the edge of the gondola and called for the spies to stop what they were doing. The woman ceased weeping and gazed up at the gondola with hope in her eyes.

"Come back," Krokur called. "We'll spare this home. It appears we've already found our quarry."

He turned back to Asa. "Can you guess where we're going next?"

She shook her head.

"We're taking you to Castle Crag."

The journey was long, and Asa had to take deep breaths to stop her panic from building. The gondola was lowered again on the field in front of the castle, and Asa was subjected to her first real look at the terrifying building. It was tall and mighty, a great hulking block. But no, when she looked closely, Asa could see that the walls bulged slightly, giving the impression of a toad that had puffed itself out to appear more frightening.

Eleven iron-gray towers scraped the sky. The rest of the building was black, but not because it had been painted black. Rather, the unfinished stone had been grown over with weeds and algae.

Asa scanned around her. She hadn't given up hope of escape, but the field they had landed in was surrounded by high walls, topped with glistening spikes.

"What shall we do with her?" Beini asked Captain Krokur. "Prepare her for meeting Flood?"

"No," Krokur replied. "She's not going in the main entrance. Take her by cart through the sinners' entrance."

"What's the sinners' entrance?" she asked, her blood running cold.

"The entrance to the dungeons," Krokur said, and the cruel twist of his lips revealed the delight he took in her fear. "The dungeons where your parents disappeared, just as you shall. Take your last look at the sky, Princess."

They herded her on a cart, pulled by a sad gray donkey. The driver was a tall, bald woman with tattoos

on her head. She said nothing as the cart began to move across the field and down a steep slope. Asa caught a glimpse of the rocky beach beyond the walls and saw *Northseeker* dumped there on her side. The ship's magical invisibility didn't work out of the water. She did what Krokur had suggested and looked at the twilight sky: pale and streaked with gray clouds. Would she ever see it again?

Then the cart passed under a gate and the sky was gone. Guards came for her, carrying her farther and farther down into the castle. The darkness closed in and the air was dank and bitter. Flickering torches lit the way. Nobody spoke to her, and she found she was too frightened to speak or protest. So they continued in silence down to the dungeons. The cold grew intense, and Asa was glad for her fur cloak.

Finally there was the grating noise of a door being opened. Her hands were unbound and she was thrust into a dark cell. The door was slammed and locked. She listened as the guard's footsteps faded and she was left alone in this awful place.

There was a movement behind her. Perhaps she was not alone after all. She peered into the gloom. "Who's there?"

"Asa? Is that you?"

The voice was familiar, but she couldn't place it. "Who is it?"

"I'm surprised you don't remember me. It's your fault I'm here, after all." Then a figure stepped out of the shadows and into the weak firelight.

It was Margritt, the witch princess. And she was extremely angry.

CHAPTER 5

THE SEA DUNGEONS

"M-Margritt," Asa stammered. "I didn't...it wasn't... we couldn't have done anything, we..." She trailed off and eyed Margritt nervously. Without her shining jewels and fine clothes, the witch princess looked even more savage. Asa couldn't think of anything to say. Margritt was right: it was her fault that the witch princess was here. When Asa and Rollo had gone to rescue Una, Margritt had been captured by a sky patrol.

Margritt stared at Asa for a long time without blinking. Then she reached out and pulled the girl's cloak from her shoulders.

"What are you doing?" said Asa, grabbing at her cloak.

"I'm cold."

"But that's mine."

Margritt wrenched the cloak away and settled it around her own shoulders. "I'm stronger than you, child. If I want your cloak, I'll take your cloak. You sacrificed me to save yourself, and now I'm doing the same."

The cold in the dungeons was icy. Asa lurched forward to snatch her cloak, but Margritt struck out with her arm and Asa was knocked to the floor.

"It's mine now. And every meal that comes in for you will be mine, too."

"But I'll starve! I'll die of cold!"

"It will be all my pleasure to watch that happen." Margritt turned and disappeared back into the shadows in the far corner of the cell.

Shivering, Asa wrapped her arms around herself. She could no longer fight back her tears, so she put her head on her knees and sobbed.

The drain was a tight fit. Sometimes Rollo swam, his hands moving under him like a frog's; sometimes he wriggled on his belly through narrow bends. The water was heading the other way, so he was swimming against the current, too. Within five minutes he was exhausted. He stopped, rested a minute, then kept going. Five minutes of swimming, one minute of rest, and so on, until almost an hour had passed. That was when he came to the blockage.

Of course, he should have been prepared for it. Prisoners must have attempted to escape over the years, but to find an entire human skeleton blocking his way was still a terrible shock.

The gray bones were curled up, knees to chest and head tucked in, almost as though it were sleeping. The drain water coursed through the ribs without slowing. But there was no way Rollo could get past.

Unless he moved the skeleton.

He swam up close. The skull was the problem. It was jammed tight between other bones, which were in turn pressed up against the walls of the drain. If he could loosen the skull...

Tentatively, he reached out. He put his fingers in the eye sockets and pulled. Nothing happened. He pulled again. It came free and he threw it behind him. The rest of the skeleton loosened, and by pulling on the spine, he was able to clear the way a little. There still wasn't quite enough room for him to get past. He tried to wriggle through the gap, but couldn't. He backed up, pondering what to do next.

And then the skeleton moved.

At first he thought it was only the water current dislodging it. One of the bony arms lifted and hit the ceiling of the drain. But then the arm moved again and seemed to point at him. His blood ran cold. The skeleton put its hands on the floor of the drain and propelled itself forward. Rollo began to wriggle backward. There wasn't enough room to turn around. This wasn't a skeleton at all; it was some kind of drain creature, and it was furious with him for removing its head.

Rollo didn't know what to do. There wasn't room to get past the creature, and he couldn't move backward as fast as it moved forward. This was all going wrong. By now, he'd hoped to have found Asa. Instead he was exhausted and being chased by a headless skeleton backward down a drain.

Something struck his foot, and at first he thought there might be another drain creature behind him. But he glanced around and saw it was the skull of the skeleton, stuck on a bend in the drain. He reached out with his toes and kicked the skull forward, underneath him, where he grasped it with his hands.

"Here!" he said, presenting the skull to the drain creature. "Is this what you're looking for?"

The skeleton paused, and Rollo felt his heart slow.

"I'm sorry," he said, offering the skull again.

The drain creature's hands shot out and snatched

the skull from Rollo's hands. With an angry movement, it jammed the skull back onto its spine and clapped its bony hands. In an instant, it had vanished.

Rollo took a moment to collect himself. Then he started moving forward again. His relief at the drain skeleton's disappearance had given him new energy. He pushed himself hard, and the drains began to widen. Within half an hour, they were tall enough for him to walk on his knees if he wanted, and the water ran through the lower half only. Rollo kept swimming, though. As soon as he breathed air again, his enchantment would wear off and he would get sick. Or worse…

But he couldn't think about that now. He had to find his sister.

Above him, every hundred feet or so, there were large grated openings. Wondering what was up there, he swam on his back. Mostly it just looked dark, but then he saw one opening with dim light struggling through it. He took a breath and rose to his knees, peered into the darkness, and listened. Nothing.

He slid back into the water and swam a little farther. Another grate. He rose and listened again. This time he heard something… somebody crying.

It was Asa!

He was about to call out when a big black foot came thundering down on the grate. Rollo sank back under the water, trying to make out the shape above him. It was a fat guard, and he hadn't seen Rollo. Quietly, slowly, Rollo rose again to peer through. He could see that the guard wore a belt of chains and that on it was a large rusted key. Rollo reached for his magic rope, unrolled the end, and said quietly, *"Koo-weee-ince, kweee-koo."*

Nothing happened.

He tried again, but this time he doubted that he had said the magic words right. The more he worried what the magic words were, the more confused he became. Frustrated, he wrapped the magic rope around his waist again and sank under the water to think.

If he couldn't use magic, he'd have to try something else. He felt in his pocket for pebbles. This was it.

He was climbing out of the water now, and the sickness would hit him within minutes. He had very little time to set Asa free.

He got to his knees, tossed a pebble up through the grate, and heard it land on the dungeon floor. The guard, made curious by the noise, stepped off the grate to go and investigate. Rollo pushed the grate. It was made of heavy iron, and he had to push hard, but it came free. He stood up in the dungeon, just as the guard turned and saw him. The guard ran toward him and Rollo heaved the massive grate at him. A corner caught the guard's stomach and he fell over, groaning.

Rollo didn't waste a second: he knelt to prize the key off the guard's belt, avoiding a meaty hand as the guard tried to grab him. Finally Rollo tossed the key at the narrow window in the cell door closest to him. It sailed through and clattered to the ground inside.

"Asa!" he called. "The key!"

The guard had Rollo by the shoulders now and was hauling himself to his feet. The cell door burst open, but it wasn't Asa who stepped out. It was Margritt. The guard closed his hands around Rollo's throat, and Rollo knew Margritt would never help him.

But he was wrong. She wanted her freedom more than she wanted revenge on the children. She picked up the grate, crashed it over the guard's head, and knocked him out.

Asa emerged from the cell, pale and shaking. Rollo's stomach began to clench with nausea as the enchantment finally wore off.

"Rollo!"

"Quick, children!" Margritt said, lifting the guard under his arms. "He's out cold, but he'll come round soon enough. Get him into the cell."

Rollo took one of the guard's legs and Asa took the other, and they dragged him into the cell. Margritt locked the door and slid the key into her pocket. She walked briskly in the other direction.

"Wait!" Asa called. "Where are you going?"

"Home."

"Do you know where our parents are?"

Margritt turned, slipped the bearskin cloak off her

shoulders, and tossed it back to Asa. Her mouth was set in a hard line, and she raised a slender finger and pointed behind them into the dark. "That way. The labyrinth."

"Can we have the key?" Rollo asked.

"No. I might need it to get out. Besides, you'll need more than a key to bring them back." She stalked away.

"Wait!" said Rollo.

"Be quiet, you little fools," she hissed over her shoulder. "Head into the dark. You'll find their cell, but you might not find your parents."

"What does that mean?"

Margritt wouldn't answer, but hurried away up the slope. Rollo felt dizzy and weak.

"Asa?" he said, but his voice seemed to come from a long way off.

"What's the matter?" she asked.

Then Rollo collapsed on the cold ground.

CHAPTER 6

THE SORCERER'S RETURN

"Rollo! Rollo, wake up," Asa said, gently slapping his face. She could hear the guard moaning in the cell. In a few minutes, he would be up and raising the alarm. "Come on, come on!"

Asa decided she would have to carry her brother, which was difficult because he was heavy. She picked him up under the arms and dragged him a few hundred feet into the dark, under a low ceiling and into the first narrow twist of the labyrinth. Then she paused to catch her breath. Rollo's eyes flickered and he sat up groggily.

"Are you all right?" Asa whispered.

"The enchantment . . . I was under it so long . . . and now I think . . ." He turned away and vomited for what seemed like ages. She rubbed his shoulder and tried not to worry too much.

"Asa," he said, turning back to her at last. "I don't feel right. I feel like I'm . . ." He trailed off and slumped forward again, unconscious in her arms. She put her hand over his chest: his heart was still beating, but his breathing was shallow and noisy. She felt overwhelmed and helpless. What if he died?

"Mother," she said under her breath. "I have to find her. She'll know what to do." But then she remembered Margritt's words: even if she found the cell, she might not find her parents. What did that mean? Were they dead after all? Was Asa doomed to lose everyone she cared about?

She couldn't let these awful thoughts weigh her

down. She eased Rollo gently onto his side and dragged him into a dark corner, where she hoped he could stay hidden until she came back.

"I love you," she whispered, and kissed his cheek. But he didn't stir. With purpose, Asa stood up and headed into the dark.

She was immediately presented with three paths, all of them unlit. She took a moment for her eyes to adjust to the dark and stretched her hand out to brush the wall. Her instincts led her to the right, but the tunnel soon finished in a dead end, so she doubled back and took the left. She hurried, straining her eyes to see anything but seeing only blackness. The tunnel curved around, and she found herself faced with another two tunnels.

Asa could have wept. She could be lost in here and never escape. She struggled to see any small sign that could help her decide. Faintly, a long way down the closest tunnel, she thought she could see light. Or maybe the endless dark was tricking her eyes. Still she had to choose, so she followed the tunnel, but was disappointed to see the light fade away the farther she advanced into the darkness.

Out in the next opening, with six tunnels to choose from now, she thought she saw it again. Then it occurred to her, perhaps there was *someone* holding the light, and that was why it kept moving away. She almost called out, but reminded herself that it might be a guard. Instead she ran as fast as she could toward the light, brushing her fingers along the wall to keep her balance. If it was a guard, her parents' prison might be nearby.

She followed the light and drew closer and closer. Sometimes it would stop for a moment, then hurry away. She rounded a bend and saw for the first time the figure that held the burning torch. It was only visible from behind, a tall man in black robes. She held her breath, watched him for a second. Then he turned slightly, and the torch lit his head in profile.

"Ragni!" she gasped.

He jumped, then turned in alarm. When he saw Asa, his face broke into a huge grin.

"Asa!"

She rushed forward and he enclosed her in a big hug. The last time she had seen Ragni, he was imprisoned on a rock in the outwaters.

"Where is your brother?" He frowned.

"He's unconscious. The enchantment... can you heal him?"

He hesitated. "I don't know."

"How did you get free?" she asked.

Ragni held out the Moonstone Star. "The magic you gave me that day. I came straight here. But I can't find your parents."

Asa's heart sank. "Oh no. They're dead?"

"I'm sure they're very much alive, but I can't find them. *You* can, though."

"I don't understand."

"Come with me." He led her back a little way into the tunnel. In the dark, Asa hadn't noticed it before, but there was a door in the wall with no window. Ragni held out his torch. "Look through the keyhole."

She crouched to look. A big, hairy beast, like a cross

between a bear and a man, lay sleeping on the floor of the cell. She stood up. "It's a monster of some sort."

"That's the only thing I see in all of these cells, Asa. Monsters, and no doubt some of them *are* monsters. But two of them are your parents."

"Flood changed them into monsters?"

"No, he can't do that. But he can enchant the key-hole so the eye is tricked." He held up the Moonstone Star, which hung around his neck. "The Star will open any of these cells, but if I open the wrong one, I release a beast that can rip me apart with its bare hands. Do you see?"

"Then how can I help?"

"You will be able to see them. The ones that love them most will be able to see through the enchant-ment if they try very hard." Ragni stroked his long black beard. "I've tried. I do love your parents, Asa. But my love is nothing like the love of a child."

Asa was overwhelmed with feelings. Fear and anxiety, but also hope.

"I wish Rollo was here to help," she said.

"If you find your mother, she can make him well again. You know that." Ragni indicated the cell again. "Look once more. Think of your parents, how much you love and miss them, and tell me what you see."

Asa peered through the keyhole. The beast had woken now and its eyes glittered in the dark. It made a grunting noise. She focused hard. So many memories of her parents had begun to fade. But then she remembered the way her father used to hold her, sitting on his knee, to brush her hair at night. He was always so much gentler than her mother, who was often busy and had to rush between one task and another. She tried to imagine whether this beast could possibly be that gentle man.

"Definitely not this one," she said.

"Let's move on."

Ragni knew all the cells, as he had been wandering here for days. They moved from one to the next. The beasts inside were all ugly and cruel-looking and often grunted or squealed at her. She went slowly and drew up feelings of love for her parents at each cell, all the time aware that she had to find them quickly. That Rollo's life might depend on her success.

"Ragni," she said, "what if it's been too long since I saw Mama and Papa? What if I've forgotten them?"

Ragni shone the torch into another keyhole. "Asa, we mustn't think about the possibility of failure. There are many, many cells down here. No guards patrol the area. We must simply keep trying, no matter how long it takes."

"But Rollo—"

"Don't think about him now. Your worry will make it hard for you to concentrate. Go on, look."

Asa bent to the keyhole. Inside, another monster. Like the others, it saw the light in the keyhole and it grunted furiously. Again, she drew her loving memories to mind and tried to identify something—anything— about this monster that reflected them.

But something odd was happening to her eyes. Her vision was blurring. The monster moved. No, it hadn't moved. Her eyes clouded over. Asa's heart began to thunder. The monster was shivering, disappearing. It wasn't a monster at all.

"Papa!" she screamed, falling back from the door.

Ragni lunged forward, catching her with one hand while he held the Moonstone Star to the door. There was a flash of blue light, the lock clicked, and the door was flung open. In a second, she was wrapped in her father's arms.

"Asa, my sweet girl," he said, stroking her hair. Her cheek was pressed against his chest and his voice boomed loudly as he said, "Ragni, the Star Queen is in the cell directly behind this one."

Ragni hurried off, and an instant later, Asa looked up to see her mother. Tears poured down her face for the second time that day, but this time they were tears of joy.

CHAPTER 7

ESCAPE FROM CASTLE CRAG

Rollo became aware of a bright light nearby. He was too weak to open his eyes, and his stomach still cramped and rumbled. But the bright light seemed to be sinking into his body and making him feel better.

"Rollo?" a soft voice was saying. At first he thought it was Asa. "Rollo, can you hear me?"

Then his eyes opened wide. He was looking at his mother.

"Mama!" he gasped. "Is this a dream?"

Her serene brown eyes gazed down at him. The Moonstone Star glowed blue around her neck. "No, my darling. It's real."

All around him was noise—the voices of his father, his sister, and Ragni as they quickly explained to him what had happened. He was stunned. He had dreamed about this moment for so long, and now that it was here, he couldn't believe it. Perhaps it was just a dream. It was too wonderful to be real.

But then a dark shadow moved in.

Rollo looked up. Standing there, a burning torch in his hand, was Emperor Flood himself.

He looked different from the way Rollo remembered. Fatter and balder, with heavy-lidded eyes. He was dressed in white, adorned with countless jewels that reflected the fire he held aloft. But all his finery couldn't hide the fact that he was just a man, and Rollo wasn't as afraid of him as he had been.

"Flood," Mama said, climbing to her feet. "Let us pass. Your game is over."

"It was never a game," Flood replied, and flung out his right hand. A zap of white-hot light jumped from his fingers to Ragni's heart and the sorcerer fell dead on the ground.

Enraged, the Queen clutched at the Moonstone Star. "You will regret that," she thundered. A second later, a pulse of blue light slammed into Flood. He staggered, but righted himself quickly and moved into the space between the children and their parents.

"Your children are clever," he said. "Perhaps I should kill them next."

The Queen held up the Moonstone Star, and Flood wagged a finger in warning. "Uh-uh, madam. You put the Star down, or I will finish them off."

She froze, and King Sigurd hung on to her hand tightly. Rollo could see that they didn't know what to do, and Flood had raised his hands to perform some other terrible magic.

Rollo remembered the magic rope at his waist. And he remembered the magic words, too. *"Kweee-koo, koo-weee-ince!"* he shouted, and the magic rope shot

out, snaked around Flood's wrists, and tied them swiftly together.

The King jumped forward and knocked Flood to the ground. Without his hands, the Emperor was powerless.

"He has all your magic," the King said to the Star Queen. "Quickly, while he's down, take it back."

The Star Queen leaned over Flood and held out the Moonstone Star. Flood swore and shouted, but he could do nothing as a gushing stream of white and blue light was sucked from his hands back into the Star.

But then, as the last drop of magic disappeared into the Moonstone Star, there was an ominous rumble.

"We have to run," the King said. "His magic was holding the castle together. It's all going to collapse."

Rollo climbed to his feet and began to run. Using the Star as a compass, the Queen led the way. They hit the back wall of the labyrinth and Rollo began to despair.

"How do we get out?" he asked.

"I can make a way out," his mother said. She spread

her hands in front of the wall and blue light buzzed around them. With a graceful movement, she drew a door in the light. Once the shape was completed, the wall dissolved and they were gazing out at the gray beach. "Come on."

Rollo followed her through, with Asa and the King behind. *Northseeker* lay on her side on the stony beach.

"All together!" their father shouted, and they began to drag the ship down to the water. Above them, Castle Crag was shuddering and shaking. Stones began to crack and tumble from the turrets, hurtling toward them with ferocious speed. One barely missed the side of *Northseeker.* Asa screamed. A small stone whizzed toward her mother and struck her on the forehead. With a mighty push, the family slid *Northseeker* into the water and they all climbed aboard.

"Rollo, you take the tiller!" his father ordered. "Asa, tend to your mother's wound."

Asa went to the storage box for bandages and gently cleaned the blood from the Star Queen's brow.

"Why are you crying, Mama?" she said. "Does it hurt?"

"Ragni was a good man," her mother said. "One of many good people Flood sacrificed."

A loud cracking sound rang out from behind them. Rollo and Asa turned. A fissure had opened up in the center of the castle wall and split wider and wider as they watched. One side of the castle began to sink.

"Go, *Northseeker*," Asa said. "When that castle comes down, we need to be far, far away."

Northseeker lurched forward, magic filling her sails. They sped over the water. The castle groaned and creaked and then, with a spectacular crash, ripped apart and fell. Flying rocks whizzed past them, peppering the water, but *Northseeker* raced away from it all, out onto the open sea. Behind them, fire and smoke filled the sky. Asa flew to her mother's arms, felt the Star Queen's warm hands on her brow and in her hair, and sobbed with relief.

A wedding is always a happy occasion, but this one is particularly special. Look around and you will see.

Katla and Skalti, dressed all in white with flowers twined in their hair, are dancing to the pipes and lutes of the royal band.

The castle is not fully dry, so the wedding is in the green front garden. The sun shines on the new daisies, and birds are singing.

A family huddles together under the low branches of an ash tree. The Star Queen has her arms around her son, Prince Rollo, while the littlest daughter, Una, toddles about, eating wedding cake. King Sigurd's head is bent to talk to his dark-haired daughter, Princess Asa, who is wearing her favorite red dress for the occasion.

The party swirls on around them. They look happy, happier than they have been for more than a year.

ABOUT THE AUTHOR

Since the publication of her first novel, *The Infernal,* in 1997, Kim Wilkins has established herself as a leading fantasy author in Australia and internationally. Her books include *Grimoire*, *The Resurrectionists*, *Angel of Ruin*, *The Autumn Castle,* and *Giants of the Frost*. She has also written a series for young adults about a psychic detective. She lives in Brisbane, Australia.

Kim's first novel, *The Infernal,* won both the horror and fantasy novel categories of the Aurealis Awards in 1997.

ABOUT THE ILLUSTRATOR

After graduating from the University of South Australia, David Cornish took his portfolio to Sydney, where he found work with several magazines and newspapers. Three years later, an opportunity arose there to be on the drawing team of the game show *Burgo's Catchphrase*. After six years with the show, David became restless, circum-navigating the globe before returning to Adelaide, Australia.

David's bold, graphic style and fine draftsmanship have made him a successful illustrator in Australia, and in the United States he is best known as both the author and the illustrator of the fantasy series Monster Blood Tattoo.

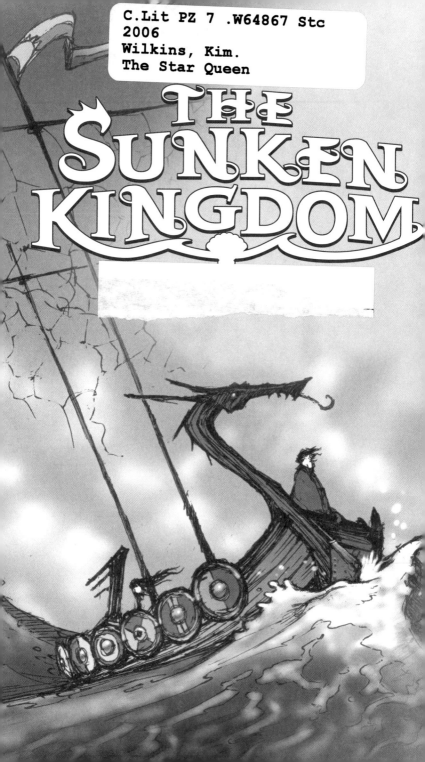